MR.
IMPOSSIBLE

by Roger Hargreaves

Mr Impossible could do the most amazing things.

For instance, Mr Impossible could jump over a house.

You try it.

It's impossible!

And Mr Impossible could make himself invisible.

All he had to do was stand there and think about becoming invisible, and he became invisible.

You try it.

It's impossible!

And Mr Impossible could fly.

All he had to do was stand there and flap his arms about, and off he flew.

You try it.

It's impossible!

And, Mr Impossible lived in an impossible looking house.

Have you ever seen a house in such an impossible place?

Of course not!

One day Mr Impossible was out walking in the woods, when he met a boy called William.

William was on his way to school.

"Hello," said Mr Impossible.

"Hello," replied William. "I'm William."

"I'm Impossible," said Mr Impossible.

"Really?" said William.

"Really," smiled Mr Impossible.

"Can you do impossible things?" asked William.

"Haven't come across anything I couldn't do," replied Mr Impossible, modestly.

William thought.

"Can you climb up that tree?" he asked, pointing to the biggest tree in the wood.

"I can do better than that," replied Mr Impossible. "I can walk up that tree!"

And he did!

William thought again.

"Can you stand on one hand?" he asked.

"I can do better than that," replied Mr Impossible. "I can stand on no hands!"

And he did!

"That's impossible," cried William.

"True," replied Mr Impossible.

Then William remembered that he was on his way to school.

"Why don't you come with me?" he asked.

"But I've never been to a school before," Mr Impossible said.

"Then it's time you did," replied William. "Come on!"

William and Mr Impossible sat at the back of William's classroom with all the other children.

The teacher came in, but didn't notice that there was somebody extra in his class that morning.

"Good morning, children," said the teacher. "I have a very difficult sum for you to do today. It will take you most of the morning to work out the answer."

And he wrote the sum on the blackboard.

It really was the most difficult sum William had ever seen in his whole life. Full of multiplications and divisions and additions and other things William didn't enjoy.

The teacher was right. It would indeed take most of the morning to work out the answer, if not most of the afternoon as well.

Mr Impossible whispered in William's ear.

William put up his hand.

"Yes, William," said the teacher. "Is there something about the sum you don't understand?"

"Please, sir," said William. "Is the answer 23?"

The teacher was very, absolutely, totally, completely amazed.

"How did you work out the sum so quickly?" he gasped. "It's impossible!"

"Nothing is impossible," said Mr Impossible from the back of the class, and stood up.

"Well I never did," exclaimed the teacher.

After that, Mr Impossible spent all day at the school.

He showed the teacher how he could read a book upside down.

"That's impossible," said the children who were watching.

"Absolutely," replied Mr Impossible.

Then William asked Mr Impossible if he would like to play in the school football match.

"Oo, yes please," replied Mr Impossible. "I've never played football before."

And do you know what he did?

He kicked the football so high into the air that when it came down, it had snow on it!

What an impossible thing to do!

Then it was time to go home.

Mr Impossible said goodbye to all the people at the school, and then said goodbye to William.

"Goodbye, Mr Impossible," said William.

"Goodbye, William," said Mr Impossible, and just disappeared.

William rubbed his eyes, and went home.

William's mother and father were waiting for him.

"Hello, William," they said. "Did you have a good day at school?"

"Yes," replied William. "And I met somebody who can do anything in the world!"

"Really William," they both laughed. "You're impossible!"

William smiled, and went inside.

And, a hundred miles away, a small figure was listening to what William's mother and father were saying.

And he grinned an impossible grin, and then he went to sleep.

Standing on his head!

And we all know, that's . . .

. . . Impossible!

3 Sixteen Beautiful Fridge Magnets – any 2 for £2.00!
inc.P&P

They're very special collector's items!
Simply tick your first and second* choices from the list below
of any 2 characters!

1st Choice

- ☐ Mr. Happy
- ☐ Mr. Lazy
- ☐ Mr. Topsy-Turvy
- ☐ Mr. Bounce
- ☐ Mr. Bump
- ☐ Mr. Small
- ☐ Mr. Snow
- ☐ Mr. Wrong

- ☐ Mr. Daydream
- ☐ Mr. Tickle
- ☐ Mr. Greedy
- ☐ Mr. Funny
- ☐ Little Miss Giggles
- ☐ Little Miss Splendid
- ☐ Little Miss Naughty
- ☐ Little Miss Sunshine

2nd Choice

- ☐ Mr. Happy
- ☐ Mr. Lazy
- ☐ Mr. Topsy-Turvy
- ☐ Mr. Bounce
- ☐ Mr. Bump
- ☐ Mr. Small
- ☐ Mr. Snow
- ☐ Mr. Wrong

- ☐ Mr. Daydream
- ☐ Mr. Tickle
- ☐ Mr. Greedy
- ☐ Mr. Funny
- ☐ Little Miss Giggles
- ☐ Little Miss Splendid
- ☐ Little Miss Naughty
- ☐ Little Miss Sunshine

*Only in case your first choice is out of stock.

--- TO BE COMPLETED BY AN ADULT ---

To apply for any of these great offers, ask an adult to complete the coupon below and send it with the appropriate payment and tokens, if needed, to MR. MEN OFFERS, PO BOX 7, MANCHESTER M19 2HD

☐ Please send ____ Mr. Men Library case(s) and/or ____ Little Miss Library case(s) at £5.99 each inc P&P

☐ Please send a poster and door hanger as selected overleaf. I enclose six tokens plus a 50p coin for P&P

☐ Please send me ____ pair(s) of Mr. Men/Little Miss fridge magnets, as selected above at £2.00 inc P&P

Fan's Name _____

Address _____

_____ **Postcode** _____

Date of Birth _____

Name of Parent/Guardian _____

Total amount enclosed £ _____

☐ **I enclose a cheque/postal order payable to Egmont Books Limited**

☐ **Please charge my MasterCard/Visa/Amex/Switch or Delta account** (delete as appropriate)

Card Number

Expiry date ___ / ___   **Signature** _____

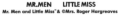

MR.MEN   LITTLE MISS
Mr. Men and Little Miss™ & ©Mrs. Roger Hargreaves

CUT ALONG DOTTED LINE AND RETURN THIS WHOLE PAGE